*To Marie-Jo
and her young writers and illustrators in the making!
It is thanks to her and her kindergarten class
at the Camille Claudel school in Triel-sur-Seine
that the idea to write about Matisse's work came to me.*

*With the help of all her kindergartners,
the first draft of this story came to life…*

*CONGRATULATIONS
Lisa, Maëlly, Margaux, Mathis, Alice, Jade, Karla, Capucine,
Antoine, Coumba, Andriana, Thomas, Gabriel, Julie,
Léane, Morgan, Andréa, Lohan, Maëlle, Nathan and Térence!*

*And THANK YOU Marie-Jo!
V.M.*

Prestel Publishing Ltd.
14-17 Wells Street
London W1T 3PD

Prestel Publishing
900 Broadway, Suite 603
New York, NY 10003

Library of Congress Control Number: 2016936143

Translated from the French by: Agathe Joly
Copyediting: Brad Finger
Project management: Mareike Rinke
Production management: Astrid Wedemeyer
Typesetting: textum GmbH, München
Printing and binding: TBB, a.s.
Paper: Condat matt Périgord

FSC MIX
Aus verantwortungs-
vollen Quellen
FSC® C022120
www.fsc.org

Verlagsgruppe Random House FSC® N001967

Printed in Slovakia

ISBN 978-3-7913-7265-5
www.prestel.com

VÉRONIQUE MASSENOT

# The MERMAID and the PARAKEET

VANESSA HIÉ

**Prestel**
Munich • London • New York

There once was an ocean, wide and beautiful,
and it had everything an ocean should.
Islands and boats! Fish and shellfish! And even... a mermaid
swaying across the bottom, among the seaweed and corals.

One day a storm came,
so loud and so strong,
with all it could contain
of anger and rage.

The wind began to blow madly,
the clouds to swell, swell, swell
and the thunder to roar, roar, roar!
Amidst the darkness of the sky
appeared thousands of gold lightning bolts.

The storm was getting out of control. Luckily,
all the boats had come safely back to harbor,
and the islands were laying low.
Underneath the water, everyone was trying to hide:
the shellfish in the sand and the fish in the rocks.
But the mermaid, alas, could find no shelter.
Not even something to hold on to.
So, the floods took her away....

The storm, in its wrath,
pushed the waves onto the shore.
The ocean was overflowing: the beach, the forest...
everything was flooded!

When the storm began to quiet down,
the water slowly pulled back.
The sun came out of the clouds and gently began
to dry the foliage on the trees. But… poor little mermaid!
The waves had dropped her on top of a tree branch. Without
any legs, how would she ever manage to get down?

As she was looking down,
the mermaid saw strange animals flying around her.

"They have wings," she thought. "They must be birds.
How beautiful they are!"
All alone on her branch, the fish-woman
felt her heart throb.
How frightening it was to be so far
from the water...
but how delightful, too. She could now discover
the jungle and the warmth of its colors!

One of the birds approached her:
"Greetings, gentle lady. I am the prince of
the parakeets. And you, who might you be?"

The mermaid introduced herself and told him her story.

"Alas, with my fish tail, I cannot reach the sea...
and without any water, I will not survive."
A tiny tear, made of gleaming mother-of-pearl,
rolled down her rosy cheek.

The parakeet felt his heart tighten.

"What misfortune! I may be a prince, but I remain only
a small bird," he thought. "How could I save her life?"
The mermaid's despair distressed him.
Full of compassion, he flew to her and perched
himself on top of her shoulder.

**T**hen, something incredible happened:
In a burst of feathers and colors,
the small parakeet turned into a
strong and handsome bird-prince!

The prince took the mermaid under
his wing and carried her down from the tree.
He then began to walk at a swift pace,
as if he had always known
how to walk like a man.

"I know a place," he said, "where
a waterfall flows. I will take you
to it and you will be saved."

From this day on and forever after,
it is said that near a clear and pure stream,
a woman with the tail of a fish
and a man with the wings of a bird
love each other with tender and blended hearts.

# The MERMAID and the PARAKEET

*Henri Matisse*

1952-1953, gouache cut out, 337 x 768.5 cm, Stedelijk Museum Amsterdam collection

# Henri Matisse

## WHO IS HENRI MATISSE?

Born in Le Cateau-Cambrésis, France on December 31, 1869, Henri Matisse did not at first seem destined to become an artist. Neither his background — his father was a grain merchant — nor his study of law had much to do with painting. But in 1890, an attack of appendicitis changed his life. During his recovery, Henri's mother gave him a painting kit... and it was an inspiration! He soon studied art at the École des Beaux-Arts in Paris in the studio of Gustave Moreau, making copies of old master paintings at the Louvre museum. He also tried his hand at a style of art called Impressionism, making sketches of nature in the outdoors. In 1898, Matisse spent time on the island of Corsica, discovering the vibrant colors of the Mediterranean. From then on, he adopted a very open style and a bright color palette. The exhibition of his paintings at the Salon des Indépendants in 1905 was a true turning point: The intensity of his pure colors and the simplification of his shapes amazed the audience. A new painting style, Fauvism, was born. From then on, Matisse would never stop making art. He travelled to Algeria, Italy and Morocco, and then settled in Collioure, France in 1914. There he created one of his famous goldfish paintings and became interested in Cubism, a style that portrayed people and objects as broken-up shapes. Matisse also introduced the idea of color oppositions in his work, such as using the color black to create light. After 1941, when an illness helped make him wheelchair-bound, Henri began to make collages out of watercolor (or gouache) and cut-out paper shapes. His most famous collages were compiled in a book called *Jazz* and a series of books called the *Blue Nudes*. Henri died at age 84, on November 3, 1954. But the "Matisse style" remains famous all over the world today.

## WHAT IS THE MATISSE STYLE?

Matisse's style is an explosion of color! His bright works may look simple, but they took many hours and days of hard work to achieve. Henri emphasizes shapes, flattens space, and prefers to experiment with the thickness of his paint than with traditional shading and toning. Arranged in patches and often outlined with black, his colors seem to burst off the canvas. Matisse illustrates in this way the joy of living and creating. Dance, music, nature, and the art of the Far East (especially Japan) are among the things that inspired him.

## THE GOUACHE CUT OUTS

When he was in his seventies, Matisse changed the way he made art. He produced collages (or découpages) from shapes that he cut out of gouache-colored paper sheets. When making these works, Henri would have his assistants pin the cut-out shapes to the wall or on a canvas until the right composition was found. "Drawing with scissors, cutting directly into color" now made up Matisse's method. "There is no break between my old painting and my découpages," Matisse said, "only a greater degree of abstraction." *The Parakeet and the Mermaid* illustrates Matisse's words. It's a huge découpage with two silhouettes representing a mermaid on the right and a parakeet on the left. Among them are a multitude of leaves and fruits, which have shapes and colors (green, blue, red and orange) that seem to dance on a white background. This remarkable artwork is similar to other collages that were inspired by Henri's visit to the tropical island of Tahiti in 1930. While there, Henri was captivated by the water in a lagoon. In this unique pool of light, the line between sky and ocean became forever blurred. Matisse uses *The Parakeet and the Mermaid* to unite sea and sky in his own way.

## WHERE CAN WE SEE WORKS BY MATISSE?

Everywhere in the world! In France, two museums are dedicated to his work: the museum in Cateau-Cambrésis, his birthplace, and a museum in Nice. You can also see his works at the Musée d'Orsay, the Centre Pompidou and the Musée de Grenoble, all in Paris, as well as in museums throughout Europe, the United States and Canada.